Barramundi Fishing Story

Arlaminga

Margaret James

Illustrated by Tiwi College Students:
Ruby Brooks, Maletta Warrior Rioli, Jayden Alimankinni,
Martine Puruntatameri, Crystal Butler, Demaga Warrior
and their Art teacher Anne McMaster

Thank you to all the Northern Territory students who inspired us with their fishing stories, especially
Francis, Caitlin, Marie, Bella, Alex, Kaylon, Tyson, Ben, Elijah, Ilarda, Lucas, Victor, Asharanah and **Kaylena.**

READING Tracks

This book is dedicated to the fantastic students at Tiwi College; Anne, their inspiring art teacher; the senior management – **Ian, Stuart, Sila, Ailsa** and **Brenda** - who have always been generous and supportive; Dianne (Tictac) who has shared her wealth of cultural knowledge, and been an inspiration to us for many years; Bertram Tipungwuti, Jennifer Clancy and Benita Tipiloura who shared their cultural knowledge in editing this book; Katie Sabel who helped edit this book; and all the dedicated staff at Tiwi College, without whom the making of this book would not have been possible. Thank you for always welcoming us so warmly to your wonderful school and island.

Glossary

*Please go to our website to hear these words. **www.readingtracks.com.au**

Tiwi word	English translation
Arlaminga	Barramundi
Yirrikipayi	Crocodile
Wunijaka	North West Wind
Pakitiringa	Rain
Pumurali	Lightning
Pumwanyinga	Thunder
Jamutakari	The Wet Season

It is still dark when the four excited cousin-brothers creep quietly out of the house with their handlines, lures, a small piece of fish for bait and a big bag. They don't want to wake the family because the little ones will ask to go with them. They all love to go fishing.

Alex, Ben, Victor and Elijah talk softly in English and Tiwi as they walk towards the river, looking out for snakes in the long, green grass.

By the time they reach the river bank, the tip of the orange sun is peeping over the horizon in the east.

The boys climb onto a big, round, brown rock next to the deep river. From this high point they look out for crocs and fish.

Ben points and shouts,

"Hey, look there! A big *yirrikipayi*."

The boys laugh. They see the croc on the other side of the river, drying off on the white sand. They aren't scared because it looks lazy and it's not close to them. It's far away, across the wide river.

But the big croc sees the boys and lifts its head. Suddenly it gets up and runs to the river, making a loud splash as it dives into the water.

The boys start to run, but Alex calls out,

"It's ok. *Yirrikipayi* just going back in the river where he live. But, we gotta look out for *yirrikipayi* when we fishing. One of us sit down with glass, like a mirror, on the rock, so he can see the water clear. If we see *yirrikipayi,* we just run back real fast."

8

This is **Alex's** country, that's why he teaches his cousin-brothers how to fish safely in the river. First they have to catch a few small mullet to use for bait.

Alex gets his line ready, spikes the small piece of fish from the bag onto his hook, and throws it into the water. He is a clever fisherman, and very lucky! He keeps fishing until he catches five small silvery-grey mullet which they will use for bait.

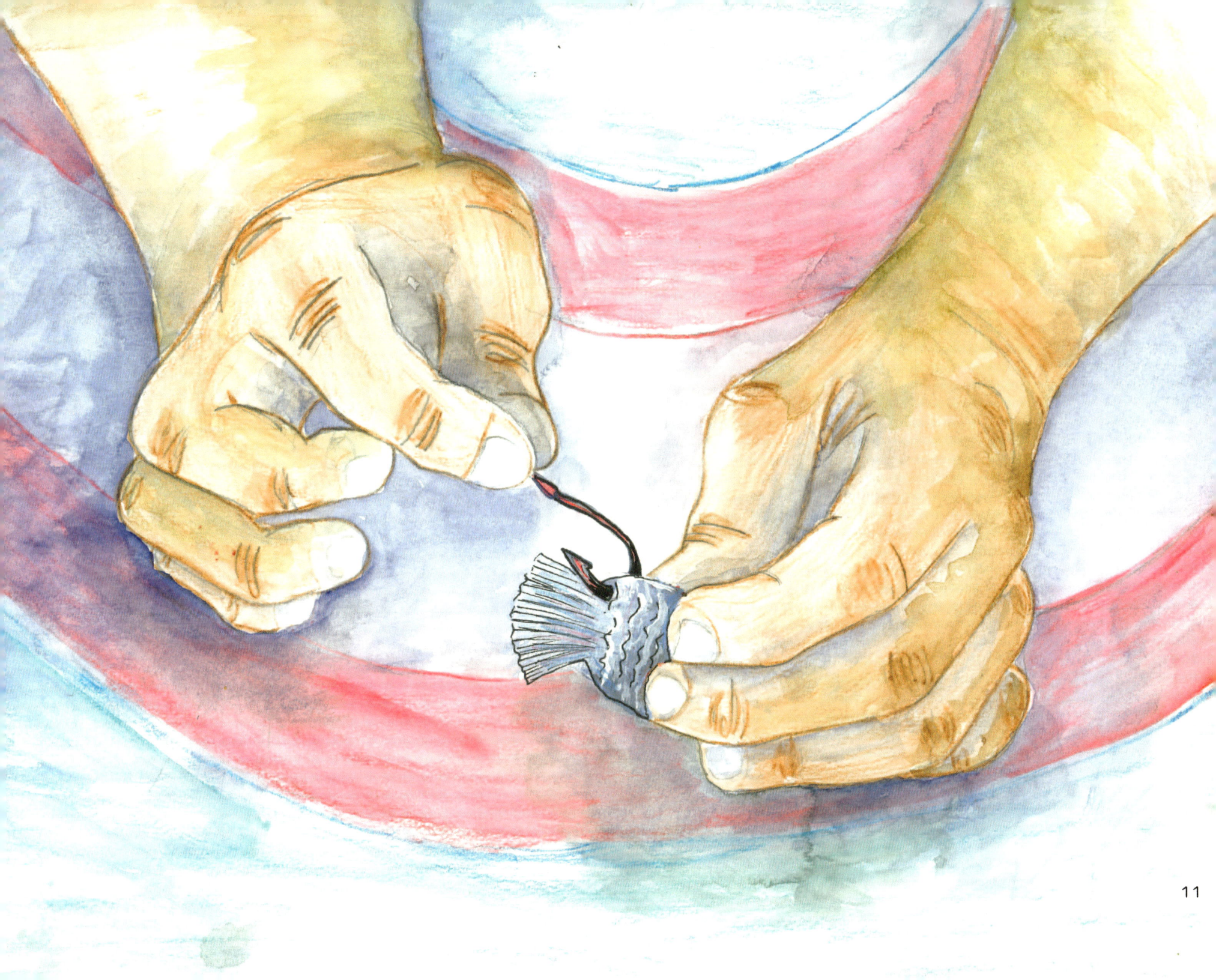

Alex says to Ben,

"Get some bait on your handline and throw it."

Ben threads his fishing hook through a mullet. Then he throws his handline. But the line goes into the water next to his feet.
They all laugh.

Alex helps Ben,

"Ben, throw it into the other side and pull it.
If it gets nothing, then just keep moving up and up until you catch one."

Ben throws his line really hard and it goes right across the river.
He holds onto his line and walks along the rocks a little way. A few minutes later he calls,

"Ey, I can feel the line pulling. It's pulling real hard. Help me Alex!"

Like an agile bush wallaby, Alex hops across the rocks to Ben, and helps him to pull in the line.

It's a big, scaly, silver barra! They put it in the bag. Alex says to Ben, who is very excited,

"Really big *arlaminga*, cousin. The family gonna be happy when we take this one home."

Arlaminga is a barramundi

13

Victor gets his hook ready and throws his line out to try for a barra. The line floats in the water for a bit, and then suddenly Victor hears a loud noise. He looks at where the line is going and he sees it is going UP into the sky, not DOWN into the water!

Alex calls out,

"Ey, what's up?"

Victor replies,

"I looked up like where the line is going and I saw it went up. Look like an eagle got the bait. Flying with it up until the trees."

Alex helps Victor. They pull the line gently, but firmly, and the beautiful, big eagle lets it go. The hook drops back down into the water, with a soft 'splash'. But the bait is missing!

Victor throws his line out again, hoping that a big, fat barra bites on his baited hook. But he has no luck.

Elijah is fishing next to Victor. He feels his line pulling and pulling, hard. He hangs on to the line and asks Victor to help him.

Victor grabs the line and they pull the fish in together. Then they notice that there is only half a barra on Elijah's line! There are big croc teeth marks on it. A croc has bitten the fish in half!

Ben and Alex run to look. Elijah says,

> "A big chunk taken out the *arlaminga*. Must have been a very big *yirrikipayi* pulling the fish on my line."

Alex says to Elijah,

> "Chuck this one back in the water. We try one more time."

Yirrikipayi is a crocodile, *Arlaminga* is a barramundi

Victor doesn't catch a fish, but he enjoys helping Elijah to catch one.

Elijah throws his line into the water again, and this time he catches a barra. He calls out,

"Ey – Alex, Ben come look! I got REALLY big *arlaminga*."

Victor helps Elijah to pull his line in, and the boys all get excited when they see the very BIG, silver-blue coloured barra caught on the hook.

Alex is proud of Elijah, and he thinks it is time to head back home now,

"The family gonna be real proud of you when they see that big *arlaminga,* Elijah. Just put it in the bag. Come on Ben and Victor, we going back to home."

The boys put the barra in the bag. The bag is heavy to carry with two big barras in it.

Arlaminga is a barramundi

The boys are hot. First they look out for crocs. Then they swim in the river.

Elijah asks Alex how he knows there are no crocs in the water.

Alex replies,

> "Because *yirrikipayi* don't just sneak out. We look out first and then when we see, we just get out of the water."

Luckily, they don't see any crocs!

They are tired, so after their swim they rest under a shady tree and yarn about their fishing.

Yirrikipayi is a crocodile

The sun is high in the blue and white sky when the boys walk back home. Clouds are beginning to gather as *Wunijaka* builds up the power to bring the afternoon *pakitiringa*. They want to get home and cook the barra before *pumurali* and *pumwanyinga* begin.

Alex is worried that the rain will come soon and make all the firewood wet. He says to Victor,

"We get grass and leaves and wood. When we get home, we get light, burn up that leaf and fire just go then. We gotta go before *pakitiringa* come."

Wunijaka is the north-west wind, *Pakitiringa* is rain, *Pumurali* is lightning, *Pumwanyinga* is thunder

Back at home, the boys scale the two big barra and clean them, while the flames of their fire burn high and hot. Alex says to his cousin-brothers,

"Take all the guts out of the fish, and clean em. We'll cook one for us now and keep one for Nana tomorrow."

The cousin-brothers relax by the fire and retell the day's events to each other, while they wait for the family to join them.

They laugh about the croc biting a barra, and the eagle taking the bait, while they watch the fire burning down to make hot ash.

Alex's Mum and big sister, Marie, come out to the fire and make damper. They mix flour, baking powder and a little bit of milk together. Then they stir in some water.

They make it into a big ball, like a pie. Mum says,

"Squash it flat like the moon, Marie."

Marie presses on the dough to make it into a big, flat circle, and then she puts it into the hot ashes.

Alex shows his cousin-brothers,

"We chuck the whole fish down on the fire, in the ash."

The barra cooks in the ashes. When the silvery skin on the fish looks dark, they flip the fish over.

The family all come to share the feed. Elijah teaches his little cousins,

"We just peel off the skin and we eat the meat. We don't eat the eyes or the skin."

As the family finish their delicious feed of damper and barra around the fire, they hear a loud *KABOOM* of *pumwanyinga* and see flashes of *pumurali*.

They grab their bags and they all run back into the house.

Pumurali is lightning, *Pumwanyinga* is thunder

There are loud claps of *pumwanyinga* and bright flashes of *pumurali*.
Then rain begins to pour down, noisily refreshing the country,
feeding the plants and filling the creeks with pure, clear water.

Jamutakari, the wet season, has begun.

Pumwanyinga is thunder, *Pumurali* is lightning, *Jamutakari* is the wet season

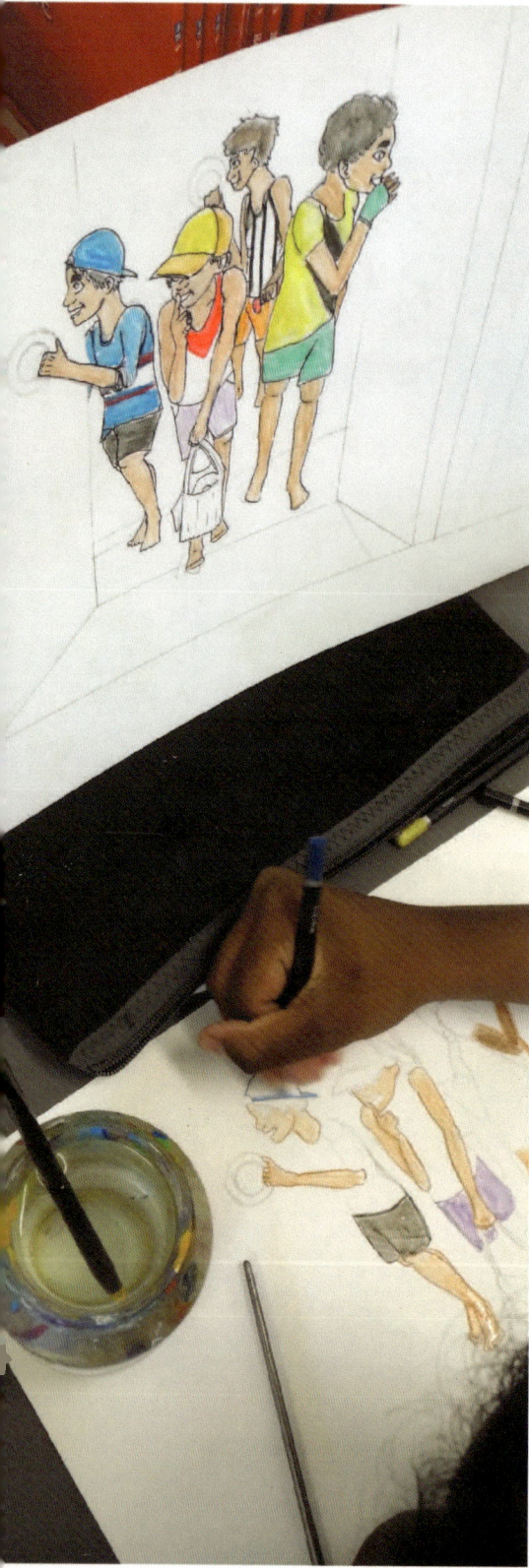

Illustrators from the Tiwi Islands, north of Darwin in the Northern Territory

Crystal Butler

I live at Garden Point or Pirlangimpi, on the west coast of Melville Island and I go to Tiwi College boarding school. My skin group is mullet. My country is Goose Creek on Melville Island. My dreaming is shark. I created 2 paintings:
1. The eagle grabbing the bait.
2. The croc grabbing the fish.

Martine Puruntatameri

I am from Millikapiti on the northern coast of Melville Island. My dreaming is jungle fowl. My skin tribe is sun and my country is Yapilika.
I painted the barra.

Maletta Warrior Rioli

I live at Garden Point or Pirlangimpi, on the west coast of Melville Island. My skin tribe is sun. My mum is Tiwi, my dad is Torres Strait. Mum's dreaming is turtle. My other dreaming is jungle fowl. My dad is crocodile and dugong. Both my parents are artists and I really like to learn from them. I painted two illustrations:
1. The barra on the fire.
2. The boys collecting wood.

Ruby Brooks

My country is Rocky Point, or Pajuwapura, on the west coast of Bathurst Island. My dreaming is rainbow serpent. My skin tribe is sun, from my mother. Every spare chance I get, I like to draw. I painted 4 pictures for this book:
1. The boys leaving the house.
2. Putting the bait on the hook.
3. The boys swimming in the waterhole.
4. The boys sitting around the camp fire.

Jayden Alimankinni

My country on Tiwi Islands is Garden Point or Pirlangimpi, on the west coast of Melville Island. My skin group is mullet. My dreaming is train. I like art and my Auntie is an artist at Tiwi Design. I would like to illustrate another book for Margaret.
I painted the croc picture for this book.

Demaga Warrior

I live at Garden Point or Pirlangimpi, on the west coast of Melville Island. My skin tribe is sun. My dreaming is turtle and jungle fowl. Maletta is my little sister. I play guitar and am also a dancer. My father is a print maker and artist from Torres Strait and my mother makes her art from home.
I painted the 2 barra in the bag for this book.

TIWI COLLEGE

Anne McMaster

Anne McMaster MFA, is a very experienced art teacher and nationally renowned artist who has been teaching art at Tiwi College for 7 years.

She says, "I'm very proud to collaborate with many of the students for this beautifully illustrated book, based on Indigenous youth and their adventures when they go hunting.

I would like to thank Margaret James for her support and the opportunity to drive this publication to fruition.

I hope you enjoy the adventures of the four young cousin-brothers communicated through the amazing illustrations by Tiwi College students."

Margaret James

Margaret James, MEd, grew up in multilingual rural South Africa with Indigenous languages surrounding her. This significantly influenced her choice of tertiary studies - among these were linguistics, languages, education, Teaching English as an Additional Language, choral conducting and voice. This background was to prove invaluable when, after a fulfilling and varied career in several countries, she moved into Indigenous Education in Australia.

Here her concern grew about the paucity of early reading material for young speakers of traditional Aboriginal languages and Aboriginal English, so she decided to do something about it. Her response was the development of the innovative and highly successful *Honey Ant Readers*, in seven Aboriginal languages as well as English, for which she has received numerous awards and accolades.

While visiting schools and communities in order to deliver Professional Development for the *Honey Ant Readers*, Margaret became increasingly aware of the similar need for engaging, early-reading material for Middle School and older learners as well. She worked closely with Elders, students and illustrators to develop linguistically and culturally appropriate learn-to-read story books for older readers. This included many unforgettable adventures out bush, learning from the Elders and children about their languages and culture, while hunting for bush tucker.

Reading Tracks ® - stories about fishing, tracking and hunting - is the result!

Jennifer Ullungura Clancy

Jennifer Ullungura Clancy

Awana! Hello and welcome. My Name is Jennifer Ullungura Clancy. I am a Traditional Owner of the Mantiyumpi land Owning Group where the Tiwi College is built.

I am excited to help launch this book for the Tiwi students and the wider Australian public to learn some stories about Tiwi life from the eyes of our Tiwi kids.

I fully support the publication of this book, as part of the *Reading Tracks* collection, and congratulate the students of Tiwi College on their wonderful illustrations.

Benita Tipiloura

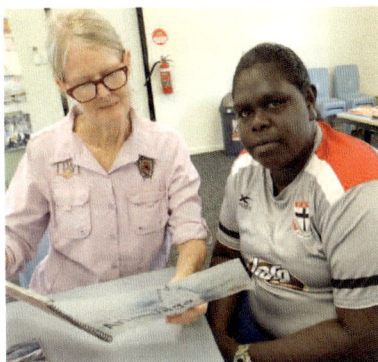

Benita Tipiloura and Anne McMaster

On behalf of my clan group, Tiwi, I welcome this book.

It'll be right for our students and families to read and learn from this *Arlaminga* book.

It's good for our young people to hear it and to learn from it, because they go out fishing with family and cousins for bush holiday.

I'll welcome kids in other parts of Australia to read this book that our Tiwi kids illustrated.

Our grateful thanks to:

All the wonderful, knowledgeable **young men and women** who shared their fantastic fishing, tracking and hunting experiences with us in the development of the *Reading Tracks* books, especially:

Agnes	Elijah	Judas	Miriam	Tyson
Alberto	Eva	Kaylena	Mitchell	Valentine
Alex	Francis	Kaylon	Ruby	Victor
Asharanah	Ilarda	Keithin	Seth	Walter
Bella	Jaika	Lane	Stanley	Zoe
Ben	Javen	Lucas	Sylvia	
Caitlin	Jess	Marie	Tamika	
Christiana	Jordan	Megan	Travis	

The **staff and students** from the schools who shared their opinions on topics for the *Reading Tracks* books with us in the early stages; shared their tracking, hunting and fishing experiences to assist us with content; and gave us important feedback on the books in the later stages of their production. Their support and encouragement were invaluable. They include:

Tiwi College, Melville Island, Tiwi Islands, NT	Ngaanyatjarra Lands School, WA
Yirara College, Alice Springs, NT	Marrara Christian College, Darwin, NT
St Philip's College, Alice Springs, NT	Kormilda College, Darwin, NT
St John's Catholic College, Darwin, NT	Alice Outcomes, Alice Springs, NT

Our many **cultural advisors** for sharing the wealth of their cultural knowledge and experience with us, and for their enormous and on-going support and encouragement, especially:

Jennifer Ullungura Clancy	Daisy Tjupamtarri Ward
Benita Tipiloura	Jennifer Inkamala
Margaret Kemarre Turner OAM	Lizzie Marrkilyi Ellis
Benedict Kngwarraye Stevens	Mervyn Japanangka Rubuntja
Marjorie Nyunga Williams	Rhonda Inkamala
Amelia Kngwarreye Turner	Trudy Inkamala
Coralie Nampitjimpa Williams	Vincent Forrester

Barramundi Fishing Story, Arlaminga, set on the Tiwi Islands, is part of the *Reading Tracks*® series of Australian fishing, tracking and hunting stories. The many accounts of fishing shared with Margaret by young fishermen and women in high schools in the Northern Territory, were the inspiration for this story.

An exciting aspect of this book about fishing for barramundi, is its illustrations by a group of very talented Tiwi teenagers, under the tutelage of renowned artist Anne McMaster, their art teacher at Tiwi College on Melville Island.

Aboriginal English and Tiwi are included in the dialogue in this book to keep the characters authentic and to draw attention to the ancient languages still spoken in Australia. Colloquial Standard English is used in the narrative to make it accessible to readers who speak English as an additional language. (Tiwi is spoken on Bathurst and Melville Islands, the two inhabited Tiwi Islands north of Darwin, in the Northern Territory. Aboriginal English is a dialect of English which is widely spoken by Indigenous Australians.)

The *Reading Tracks*® books grew out of a desire to provide relevant and culturally affirming stories for Middle School and older Indigenous literacy learners - books that would engage them. At the same time, everyone involved in the production of these books hopes that all young Australians will learn a bit more from them about the First Australians' ancient cultures and practices of food gathering.

The Elders involved in the development of these books, and the many students who wanted to share their stories, expressed their desire to have books about true stories, fishing, traditional bush tucker skills, and the old ways of tracking and hunting. In order to achieve this, Margaret worked very closely with Elders and students, going on bush trips and yarning about tracking, hunting and fishing for many hours, to ensure that the stories were culturally accurate. Elders edited the books to confirm that they were appropriate for publication, and students gave their feedback after reading them.

Join *Reading Tracks*® on a cultural journey through the beautiful landscapes of the Australian central deserts and the northern rivers, oceans and islands.

Assisted by funding from

Australian Government
Department of the
Prime Minister and Cabinet

© 2018 Margaret James
Visit us at: www.readingtracks.com.au
Email: info@honeyant.com.au
Published by Honey Ant® Readers Pty Ltd
www.honeyant.com.au
Published 2018
Design & layout by Kathy Mason

ISBN 978-1-925855-32-6

NATIONAL LIBRARY OF AUSTRALIA — A catalogue record for this book is available from the National Library of Australia

® *Reading Tracks* is registered at the Australian Trade Marks Office by Margaret James

CPSIA information can be obtained at www.ICGtesting.com
Printed in the USA
BVIW121046051118
532206BV00010B/23